THE REALM: WARFARE

THE REALM
WARFARE

A continuous journey

BY A-LEIGH ANN

Charleston, SC
www.PalmettoPublishing.com

The Realm: Warfare

First Edition

Hardcover: 978-1-68515-559-9
Paperback: 978-1-68515-560-5
eBook: 978-1-68515-561-2

DEDICATION

To the saints who showed me what the love of Christ looks and feels like—I couldn't have written this without you. I pray the fruit of your labor brings God more glory.

Grace and peace.

To my family, who introduced me to Jesus—it may have taken me twenty-four years to follow him, but you planted the seeds that grew into my faith.

Keep sowing seeds.

To my husband, thank you for your leadership and for pushing me to continue in the race.

I love you.

TABLE OF CONTENTS

PROLOGUE

She is lying on the ground, blood pouring out of her rib cage. The blood and the wound dissolve as she looks down at her torso. She gets up and feels no pain. She is limping but doesn't see the damage that has been done to her.

PART 1

DISCOVERING SHE CAN

CHAPTER 1

THE JOURNEY BEGINS

This is not your average story about your average girl. In fact, I am quite unaverage, pretty much unknown—but I know you're there. I used to stand on the back porch and dream, dream of a place to fit in.

She thinks back to when she was nine and lived in Nebraska. The sunset was so beautiful. Shades of red, pink, and orange mixed perfectly into the sky. In the distance, golden rays of light shone on the normally beige-colored office buildings at Offutt Air Force Base.

Life is a journey. A journey of discovery, a journey of highs and lows, a journey to success, a journey of—well, whatever you want life to be. My journey? I have no idea. I have no real plan; if I do have a plan of some kind, I have no idea how I'm going to get to its end point. And if I get there, will it even be enough? What is enough? So many people strive toward goals their whole lives—what happens when you reach them?

If you gain all the money, popularity, fame, prestige, or accolades you can have in this life, is that really going to be enough? Is the purpose of my life to keep pursuing these goals, these things that seem so far out of my grasp that I hesitate at the thought of trying to attain them? I hesitate because I know they won't satisfy me.

Deep thoughts on a Monday morning as I prepare to go to physio psychology.

She closes her journal, picks up her backpack, and walks toward the science center. The sun illumines her green and yellow sorority jacket. The Greek letters *Pi Chi Xi* are fading from a crisp white to the beginnings of a soft cream.

By the way, I am Makriá Daras(h)—the h *is silent. Most call me Kree. Please don't ask me how I got those names; to my knowledge, there is no Greek or Hebrew heritage in my family, just good ole Southern African American. It is my last year of college, and so many changes are coming my way. I am graduating soon—and unfortunately have to be an adult now. Yay, bills, bills, and more bills. Thankfully, I have a job lined up. I'm going to serve my country in the air force—Commissioned Officer Kree. Definitely didn't see myself in the military, but scholarships are pretty persuasive.*

I am president of the distinguished chapter Phi Tau of the amazing Pi Chi Xi Sorority Incorporated, serve as secretary on the student government board, and have a 3.8 GPA, a boyfriend, and a loving family. Most people on the outside looking in would say I have a pretty good life. I do, but it's not enough.

Kree looks up from her journal as Ray, Kree's sorority sister, sits down with her in the cafeteria. "Kree, you are looking exceptionally gorgeous in your green and yellow today." Ray tosses her backpack onto one of the chairs, and her phone lights up. "Girrrllll, you remember John of Rho Chi Delta?"

Kree rolls her eyes on the inside and thinks, *Another day discussing these random guys I do not care about.* She responds, "No, girl, what happened?"

Ray swipes at her phone. "Well, he is supposed to be dating Shay, but I saw him at the Gamma party with Dessie."

Kree looks at the picture. "Well, they look like they know each other really well…I thought he was supposed to be dating Cassidy?"

"Yeah, about that—Cassidy and Shay had a fight because Shay went after him, knowing that Cassidy had started talking to him."

Mental note: do not date Greek guys. Good thing my boyfriend is not Greek.

"I guess there is no loyalty. I thought Shay and Cassidy were friends…and they are fighting over him? And he is with someone else?" Kree says.

"Girl, I know—can't trust any of 'em…anyways, you coming to the party tonight?"

Kree responds unenthusiastically, "You know I will be there."

It's the night of the party. Midnight. All the college kids and predators are on the prowl. Guys are leaning over girls trying to take them home. Two guys are kicked out for starting a fight. Kree arrives with her sorority sisters. They step in; it's dark and smoky. Someone gives Kree a drink. Normally she has fun drinking and partying, but tonight is different.

She looks around and thinks to herself, *What is the point of it all? Guys trying to hook up with girls, girls trying to hook up with guys.* A guy tries to pull Kree to dance with him, but she declines; he angrily walks off. *And if I don't dance, people get mad...sir, I don't even know you.* Lost in her thoughts, Kree sits down as her friends venture off into the club.

Kree texts her boyfriend, Alan. "I miss you...it's soo boring here, all they want to do is drink and twerk, I'm over it."

Buzz, buzz. "I told you about hanging out with them...I miss you too. Can't wait to see you this weekend," Alan replies.

Cali, one of Kree's best college friends, calls her over. *Well, I can at least pretend I want to be here.* Kree joins her friends.

It's graduation time. Kree walks across the stage, her cap nicely snug on her Afro. *This is it—the end of this chapter in my life. Has it really been four years?* Kree accepts her diploma; after the ceremony, she finds her family, and they go out to eat.

Alan stands up and in a loud voice yells, "Can I have your attention?" Kree's family looks at him. "For eight-plus years, I have gotten to know Kree, and I must say...she has annoyed me most of the time." Her family laughs as Kree rolls her eyes. "But one day I realized that through our ups and downs, there is no one else I'd rather have annoy me for the rest of my life." Alan turns to Kree and presents a ring box. "Kree, will you marry me?"

Kree looks in the box. "Where is the ring?"

Alan replies, "What if I told you that I couldn't get it yet?"

"Alan, stop playing, and give me my ring," Kree demands.

Her mother laughs and shakes her head. "What is wrong with my child?" she exclaims. Everyone congratulates the newly engaged couple.

Alan and Kree elope five days before Kree must report to her commanding officer at Joint Base Charleston. Kree leaves Alan in Charleston and goes to San Antonio for three months to train.

During some downtime, Kree and her classmates go on an eighties-themed pub crawl. They barhop, and drinks are constantly being handed to Kree. She drinks so many that she throws up in the car of one of the captains right before they take her back to her hotel room. *Uurgh, why did they give me those nasty fries? Now I've embarrassed myself and thrown up in this man's car.* Kree stumbles into her room and falls on the bed.

She wakes up, but she can't move. She wants to move but feels like something is holding her down. Her mind is groggy from drinking the night before. Whatever is holding her down feels dark. *Something is wrong*, she thinks. *I have to get up.* The more she tries to get up, the more the weight bears down on her. She is tired; her mind is foggy. *I just want it to stop.* Later she wakes up and takes a shower. *I will never get that drunk again*, she promises herself.

Back in Charleston, Kree starts feeling the same way she did her last year of college. She loves her husband, but it's not enough. She has a good job she doesn't like. But she is grateful for what she has. Her mind plays back to a phone conversation she had with her dad.

"Hey, my firstborn. How are you and my son-in-law?"

"We are good, just getting used to Charleston."

"Ah, OK. Well, hope everything is going well…remember to put God first."

"I will. Love you. Talk to you later." *I know you're there, God, but who are you?*

Enter the Realm: It is a neutral space, a white void, expansive, and without the constraint of humanly space and time. Kree, along with numerous other people, is wrapped up in a cocoon, chains holding her in place, preventing her from moving. Only her head is visible; she has the appearance of a corpse. Kree's heart starts beating slowly underneath her cocoon.

Over the next several months, Kree searches for a place that will help her find God.

CHAPTER 2

GETTING WHAT SHE DIDN'T ASK FOR

Kree gets to her office. *It's hard to believe I'm actually here in the military. An officer.* She looks around nervously. She is only twenty-two and is in charge of an office of three guys five to eight years older than her. As she is getting set up, a fellow officer stops by her door.

"Hey, Makriá, welcome to the squadron. I'm Kyle, I work in vehicle maintenance flight."

Kree gets up and shakes his hand. "Hi, Kyle," she says.

"We are about to have a staff meeting in about thirty minutes, you should stop by."

Kree goes to the meeting and is introduced to the staff. She tries to focus on what they are talking about, but there are *so* many acronyms.

After the meeting, Kyle stops her in the hallway. "So, Kree, not sure if you have plans this evening, but you and your husband are invited to come hang out with me and some friends. We are having a game night."

Kree thinks, *Well, I definitely need to find friends here; I'll ask Alan if he wants to go.* "That's sounds good, Kyle."

"Cool. I do want to let you know that they are Christian."

"That's OK."

At the game night, Kree looks around and tries to figure out whom to talk to. A lady comes up to her. "Hi, I'm Janice, thanks for coming tonight."

"Thanks for having me."

"Where are you from?"

"Nashville, Tennessee."

"And you work at the base with Kyle?"

"Yeah, I got there a few months ago."

"How do you like working there?"

"It's OK. I'm learning a lot of different things."

"That's cool; have you found a church to go to yet?"

"No, I go to different ones but haven't found one that seems…right."

"Well, we have Bible study on Mondays at my house, you're welcome to come."

"Thanks for the invite."

Kree and Alan attend a Bible study. Everyone is gathered in Janice's basement. A man is sitting in a recliner; he is in his midthirties. He seems to be the leader. He looks at everyone and says, "Should you trust what I say?"

Kree is thoroughly confused. *What is this man talking about?*

"I could be lying to you; how would you know if I weren't telling you the truth?"

Someone answers, "I guess you would have to read the Bible so you know the truth?"

"Right. So we are at a Bible study tonight, which means we are going to study the Bible." Laughter erupts among the group.

A couple of weeks and Bible studies later:

"So, Kree, have you seen this before?"

"No, I don't think I have."

Bella presents Kree with an index card that has pictures and words on it. "I like to show this to people to help them see where they are in their relationship with God; do you mind if I share it with you?"

"That's fine."

Kree watches as Bella explains the gospel of the kingdom of God to her. "Kree, if you had to choose between these two paths, which one would you say defines your lifestyle? Is it the one of the world, in which you live in sin and for yourself, or the one in which you have chosen to turn from those things and are seeking to follow God with your life?"

Kree reflects on her life. *Man*, she thinks, *I am definitely not on the path that is leading toward God. If what this lady is saying is true, I'm actually headed to hell.* "Honestly, I'm on the first path," she replies to Bella.

"Thanks for sharing. Is there anything keeping you from repenting and giving your life over to Jesus?"

Questions immediately flood her mind. *How do I know if what she is saying is true? Can I actually live free from sin? Will I actually repent and continue to turn away from sin? There are already a few sins that she identified that I feel like I will want to commit tomorrow. How will I know if I'm ready to make this type of commitment? Hmmmm, I don't know how I will be able to do it, but I trust God will help me. I really do want to follow him*, she thinks to herself.

"Nothing is keeping me; what am I supposed to do now?" Kree asks Bella.

In the Realm, Kree's cocoon is starting to get color as her heart begins to beat faster.

"Well, the first step is repentance. You must change your mind and agree that living for yourself and in sin is wrong and choose to follow after Jesus and his ways. Keep in mind that this is the first step; your decision to repent will lead you to a lifestyle change where you are continuously and actively seeking to bring God glory by turning from sin and doing his will. Are you ready for that?"

"I am," Kree responds.

"Awesome! So now I encourage you to take some time with me and pray to God. Let him know your desire to repent and follow him."

In the cocoon, Kree's heart beats faster and faster until it attains a regular heartbeat. Her eyes open.

After they are finished praying, Bella hugs Kree and exclaims, "It is really awesome that you have made this decision to follow after Jesus and his ways. Like I briefly mentioned earlier, this is the first step in having this relationship with Jesus."

"What do I do now?" Kree asks.

"Well, Kree, it's not enough just to profess your faith; you must also seek to obey God and follow his commands. Do you know what God has commanded us to do to help us live that way?"

"No," Kree answers.

"Discipleship."

"Can I be discipled?"

CHAPTER 3

STRENGTH IN NUMBERS

Kree is sitting across from Bella; they are having their first discipleship meeting. Bella asks Kree lots of questions about her life and also about things that will help her grow in her faith. Kree then discloses to Bella the main sins she has been struggling with—anger, worry, and lust/impurity.

In the cocoon, Kree is awake and tries to move, but the chains binding her will not allow her to. The more she struggles, the more tired she becomes. A figure appears, walking toward the cocoons. The figure is humanlike, with a black cloak that trails behind it. It walks past each cocoon, looking intently at the people as if it were looking for someone. The figure stops at Kree; Kree looks up at the figure and sees two warm amber-colored eyes. The figure pulls back its hood and is revealed to be a woman who resembles Bella. But she is different from Bella; she looks like her but is glowing—her skin, her eyes, her hair. She looks stronger, not with an arrogant or boastful strength but one of love, gentleness, and humility.

The Bella figure pulls a sword handle out of her pants pocket. She closes her eyes as if to pray, and a bright light shoots out of the handle and forms something that looks like a sword. The Bella figure slices the chains binding Kree as if they were made of butter.

Kree, having been freed from her chains, falls to the ground. The Bella figure catches her and helps her stand up.

Back to the meeting:

"Kree, thank you for sharing those things. I want you to know I'm here for you and I'm on your team. We talked through what is leading you to those sins. Would you agree that you no longer desire to give into them?"

"Yes."

"Do you see why it's dangerous to hold on to those sins?"

"Yes."

"Keep in mind that we are in a spiritual war. Yes, you have made the choice to follow Jesus, you've repented, and you're getting discipled. Awesome! But you must be on the alert because the devil doesn't stop attacking you. He will continue to lie to you and try to pull you away from God, even more now because he knows you are trying to follow God and his ways."

"How do I stay on the alert?" Kree asks.

"You have to know God's word and seek to apply it in every area of your life. That is why it's important for you to spend a good amount of time reading God's word and applying it. God's truth sets us free from Satan's lies and deceptions. Let's look at John 8:31–32."

In the Realm, two hooded figures are sitting cross-legged in front of each other. One is Kree, and the other is Bella. But they are different. They are glowing—their skin, their eyes, their hair. They look stronger, not with an arrogant or boastful strength but one of love, gentleness, and humility.

"The application for this lesson is to pray for three people this week," says Bella.

Kree thinks to herself, *I have to do what? I don't like talking to people.*

"And we are going to start right now by praying for that lady over there."

Bella and Kree are meeting for discipleship at a local café. Kree's heart starts racing as she approaches the woman, who is among the other customers.

"Excuse me, I wanted to know if there is any way that I could pray for you?"

"Sure. My mother is in the hospital, you can pray for her."

Kree prays for the lady and afterward feels like a weight has been lifted off her shoulders. *That wasn't so bad.*

Back in the Realm, a second hooded figure, in ash gray, appears next to Kree (they are standing). "I don't know what to say to her," the figure says.

Kree repeats, "I don't know what to say to her."

"What if I say the wrong thing or it's awkward?"

Kree repeats, "What if I say the wrong thing or it's awkward?"

The gray figure faces Kree and takes off its hood. The figure looks identical to Kree. "Not sure if I can do this." As Kree repeats what the figure has said, the figure reaches out and touches her shoulder. Fear arises in Kree, and her glow starts to fade. "This is uncomfortable."

Kree repeats, "This is uncomfortable."

Another figure emerges for a few seconds. It is talking in the ear of the gray Kree. "I don't think I can do this," it whispers.

"I don't think I can do this," gray Kree tells the real Kree.

"I don't think I can do this," Kree responds.

But Kree remembers what she learned about praying in the lesson. She finally looks at the gray Kree; the word *flesh* appears on gray Kree's forehead and disappears. Kree takes a sword handle out of her pants pocket. "I could think about how I can't pray for this lady or the fact that it would be hard, but I'm not going to let fear stop me."

Kree's sword starts to grow, and she starts glowing again. "If I think about that, I will never be able to follow God the way I desire." Her sword grows even larger. "I'm going to pray for her." Kree cuts off the arm that is attached to the hand on her shoulder, and she can now see the other figure that was talking to gray Kree; the word *lie* appears above it, and she slices this figure in two.

CHAPTER 4

MORALE

In the Realm, a group of twelve men and women are gathered; all have on dark attire. A man steps up, his uniform is different. It is reminiscent of a uniform the commander of Roman armies would wear.

He says, "You have forces actively warring against you: your flesh, the world, and the devil. Satan will use each one to distract you, hinder you, and tempt you into sin. How does Satan do this? With lies. Satan will deceive in every area in which you don't know the truth. He will use every selfish desire to tempt you to choose it over God. If you give him authority, he *will use it against you*!

"So how can we possibly win a war in which it is guaranteed that we will get attacked, tempted, and our faith tested? Should we dwell on our humanness and give up the fight?

"Friends, saints, fellow warriors in Christ, do you know why it is so important that we know the word, why we train ourselves in the word? We train so we can fight. We fight so that we can bring God's kingdom to earth, we fight to help each other continue on in the faith, and we fight so that we can help the new disciples mature in their faith. Body of Christ, everything you do or don't do, every decision that you make, affects your brothers and sisters to the left and right of you.

"Humble yourselves, deny yourselves, die to your flesh, the world, and Satan and his schemes. Fix your eyes on Jesus, and follow the example he has laid out for his followers; he is the standard of our living. He, not we, defines what is good. Repent of anything holding you back from loving God in the way he desires.

"And as you fight, as you conquer, as you destroy the schemes of the evil one, remember your armor! God has given us everything needed to fight in this war.

"Your belt of truth holds all your other weaponry together. The truth of God's word is your foundation. Your breastplate of righteousness protects your heart from desiring evil and wicked ways. Prepare your feet with the gospel of peace. Train saints—be prepared at work, at school, with family, with friends, to share the message of reconciliation, the gospel. Do not delay as the time draws near for our Lord's return, and we do not know what day or what hour he will come. Your mission field includes every area of your life; do not waste an opportunity to open the eyes of those who are perishing to the glory of Christ.

"Take up the shield of faith! Your faith reminds you of your identity, God's character and his ways, and the path that leads to eternal life. The world is temporary and will pass away; set your mind on things above! Dwell on this to shield from the attacks that try to take your focus off Christ and shift it to you, the world, and wickedness. Take up the helmet of salvation, saints! We live for the day that we will see Jesus and not for this present life. Live with that day in mind. And take the sword of the Spirit, which is the word of God! Saints, we are not to play defense in this war; we are to destroy the enemy and his lies! How do you defeat a lie? With the truth. I caution you, however, to wield your swords carefully, for even as you can use them to destroy lies, you can also hurt those whom you are trying to help in the process.

"Prepare for war, saints! Ready yourselves for battle!"

The group erupts in cheers and praises to the Lord for what he has done for them and for him equipping them to fight valiantly for his kingdom.

CHAPTER 5

HIS MAJESTY

Jesus is on the cross, blood pouring out of his body and trickling down his feet. A pool of blood is gathering at the foot of the cross. He struggles to take a breath. The soldiers are mocking him and casting lots for his clothing. He looks out and sees the sadness, the fear, in his mother's eyes. The grief that washes over her as she realizes that her son will die.

If only she understood what is taking place, he thinks, *her mourning would turn into rejoicing; she will know soon enough.*

Jesus is in the Realm. His form and stature are grander than they are in his human state. Light radiates from every inch of his skin. His eyes are like glowing embers. His skin like polished bronze. His hair as wool, as if a crown of purity has been placed on his head. He is dressed in white. A dark figure inches toward him. The figure is holding chains—*doubt, fear, discomfort, discouragement.*

He tries to get Jesus to wrap the chains around himself. "Is it worth it to die for these creatures? What have they done to deserve your sacrifice? Look at how many times God has saved them, and they rebelled against him. Look at how wicked they are. Why suffer if these people scoff and laugh at you? Torture you? Blaspheme you? Get yourself off the cross."

As the dark figure speaks, the scene turns back to Jesus on the cross.

The sound of thunder breaks the silence. Lightning shoots across the sky, and a legion of angels appears for a split second around Jesus. The angels are fierce, akin to soldiers trained for a vigorous war. They have their swords drawn, waiting in anticipation for a command. The lightning strikes again, and they disappear.

In the Realm, Jesus looks at the dark figure, and the chains dissolve. "You know you have lost. But so that my Father receives glory, I do exactly as he commands me." The dark figure tries to shoot Jesus with flaming arrows, darkened with temptations and lies, but the arrows disintegrate well before they can reach Jesus. "Your time is short," Jesus says to the dark figure. Light radiates from him like energy beams, and the dark figure is blasted away from Jesus.

Jesus lifts up his head in prayer to God, his hands stretched out like he is on the cross. The light radiating from him grows brighter and brighter.

PART 2

EMOTIONS

CHAPTER 6

A FALLEN SAINT

Kree stares at a post written in her church's group chat: "Joseph was the victim of a hit-and-run accident; he has been declared dead at the scene. We are going to pray for healing, for him to be resurrected! Meet at Jameson Place to pray for him at 6:30 p.m.; you can also pray on your own. Tyler, Garrett, and Mike will attempt to pray for him at the hospital. Saints! Have faith. God is a God of miracles!"

Kree thinks to herself, *How could this have happened? What are the odds that Joe would be hit and killed by a car?* She falls to her knees and immediately starts praying for Joe. "Lord, we know that you are an awesome God! I know that you are miraculous; I believe you can raise Joe from the dead…but I pray in accordance with your will. Lord, I pray for you to resurrect Joe, but no matter the outcome, use this situation for your good; use this situation to bring people to you. Let this situation be what people need to give their lives over to following you. Lord, show your glory."

Kree gets up and goes to work. Later she checks the group chat. There is no update.

Saturday morning she checks the chat again and sees the following words: "Saints, Joseph's funeral will be in his hometown tomorrow at 1:00 p.m. We are renting a car to go to the service. Please let me know if you want to go."

Kree and her friends walk into the funeral home. A feeling of uneasiness settles over Kree. She does not like going to funerals—they are sad, people are upset, and she cannot stand crying in public. Kree holds Alan's hand.

In the Realm, the saints have gathered together, each one on bended knee, praying to God. "It's not too late," one saint cries out.

"God can heal him!" another responds.

"Yes he can! Remember Lazarus! He was dead four days!" a third says.

The saints nod their heads in agreement. As they are speaking, dark, faceless figures start to gravitate toward them and form a circle. In the swarm of dark figures appear the words *grief*, *doubt*, *depression*, *anger*, *bitterness*, and *confusion*.

"I remember just how much life Joe had in him. He was so excited about loving God and others," a saint states.

"Yes, he was so humble and ready to lay down his life for the kingdom," another saint states. "There is still time, keep praying."

Kree lets go of Alan's hand and goes to her friends. She hugs them. "Well, I don't like the circumstances, but it is good to see the rest of the saints." Kree and her friend Jaime go into the sanctuary, and the service begins.

"I'm not going to cry, I'm not going to cry," Kree repeats to herself. A slideshow of Joe is playing on the screens, and Kree breaks down in tears. She thinks, *I really did not want to cry today. I think I understand people's grief when they lose a loved one more. I've never had someone close to me die before. I didn't see or talk to Joe a lot, and we aren't related biologically, but he was my brother.*

Kree's sadness turns to joy as the slideshow progresses. Joe was so happy in his life—not that superficial worldly happiness but true joy in Jesus. She can feel his joy through the pictures, and she remembers how content he was in her interactions with him. Up to this point, Kree has been praying for Joe to be resurrected, but while watching the slideshow, she realizes that Joe is not going to be.

"God, please use Joe's death to lead people closer to you. Bring healing to his family, and lead them closer to you as well. Unite our church body in this time of mourning. Joe was a good friend and a great ambassador for your kingdom.

I don't understand how this could happen, but Lord, use this time of mourning for your glory."

Kree looks around the sanctuary and sees her fellow brothers and sisters in Christ. All she sees are red faces, tears, sniffling. *I can't believe he is actually gone, but I am joyful because I know he is with Jesus,* Kree thinks and then tries to focus on the message given during the service.

In the Realm, some of the saints have their heads down, some are crying, some are stone-faced, some are smiling, remembering Joe. The swarm of darkness starts circling the group, targeting certain saints to pick off and attack. A figure dressed in white starts to walk toward them. The figure has on the same type of armor as the saints, but his is as white as freshly fallen snow. The figure walks up to the group and takes off his hood. The figure looks like Joe but different; it is as though he is bathed in radiant light. His skin is glowing, and his eyes glow as well with a deep amber aura.

He smiles at the group as if to say, "Don't be sad, I'm right where I want to be." Then he turns and walks in the opposite direction. It looks like he is walking on a path; the path is bright, like his clothes. On either side of it are bright green trees; the sky is a radiant blue, as if God took the color from the rainbow and painted the sky with it. Joe keeps walking until he comes to a gate. The doors open, and he walks in.

The saints start rejoicing as they see their brother finish the race! The journey! As their brother receives the greatest gift ever, to be with Jesus forever. As they rejoice, they start to glow, the circling darkness scattering. Kree walks off by herself.

Suddenly, a soft whisper emerges and then grows louder. "They are sad; some of them are asking God why this happened. Their friend has been taken from them. Why would God do this? Why would he do this to you? Doesn't he love you? Wouldn't he want you to be happy and thus bring your friend back to life?"

Kree hears these words and rejects them. "God is still good!" she yells. "We live in a broken world, our bodies are temporary, and we will all die one day. Joe no longer has to suffer. He doesn't have to fight anymore; he doesn't have to be in this world anymore."

Kree and her friends leave the funeral and go home. In the morning, Kree wakes up to spend time with God, reading in his word and praying. All she can think about is Joe and his funeral. A wave of sadness overcomes her. "Lord," she prays, "I rejoice because he is in the best place for him. I am sad that my brother is gone; please comfort me in this."

As she finishes praying, she is transported to the Realm.

A figure dressed in dark blue stands in front of her; it looks just like her. The figure reaches out and touches Kree's heart. "You are sad. Keep crying. You ask, 'Why has this happened to him?' You are sad."

A faceless black figure appears momentarily and looks like it is telling blue Kree what to say; the word *doubt* appears over it, and then it disappears.

Blue Kree's forehead reads *grief/sadness*. Kree looks to her left and sees her flesh, gray Kree, crying. Blue Kree is touching gray Kree's heart.

Kree closes her eyes and prays. "Lord, I can't think straight. I know you are good; I know he is in a better place. I just want to be close to you now."

Kree turns on her speaker, goes on the internet, and plays her favorite worship songs. The words in the songs bring her comfort. She dwells on the goodness of God as she sings praises to him. She is reminded that her hope and home are not on earth.

CHAPTER 7

ALLIES OR ENEMIES?

In the Realm, Kree and Alan stare at each other as both prepare to draw their sword for battle. They rush at each other. Their swords clash. They clash swords a couple more times and then retreat. A dark figure appears and whispers something to Kree while handing her a bow and arrow. The bow is black and iridescent, mirroring the dark cloud swarming around the figure. Kree takes it, draws, and aims at Alan. The dark figure places its hand on Kree's arm, guiding her to shoot Alan in the heart.

"They left a letter on our door threatening to evict us. I thought you paid rent." Kree lets go of the arrow, which sails toward Alan. The words *frustration*, *irritation*, and *anger* briefly appear above it. The arrow hits Alan's breastplate, creating a small hole.

A dark figure appears by Alan, giving him a bow and arrow identical to Kree's. Alan angrily responds, "You need to stop worrying!" He shoots an arrow back at her; the same words appear above it as it pierces Kree's breastplate.

Alan thinks, *If she would be quiet, I could tell her that I did make the payment. She doesn't trust me.*

A figure appears that looks like Alan, though it is red in color. "You don't deserve this. Who does she think she is?" the red figure says to Alan.

PART 3

WAR IS A VERB

CHAPTER 8

IT'S REAL

The war—relentless, unforgiving, draining. This is what we were born into. The hold sin has over us is intoxicating before we are awakened, enlightened, made aware of the enemy's plot to destroy our souls. Even in the deepest recesses of my mind, I knew what was right and what was wrong. However, the more wrong I did, the more I wanted to do it.

Don't get me wrong—your definition of "bad" or "wrong" is not the same as mine. Drunkenness, sex, jealousy, anger, a little white lie here or there—why, these are the characteristics of a normal college kid "doing her life her way." Get that degree, land that super-high-paying job, don't depend on anyone to help you, get that American Dream, your American Dream.

I lived that way, faithfully, during my college years. By all appearances, I was the epitome of good. The good daughter, going to college, joining the military, making something of herself. The good friend, as eager to turn up and get wasted as attend campus ministry the next morning. I was a saint by most people's standards. So why did I feel so empty? Why did I struggle with loneliness and later, while in the military, with depression? Why did I find solace in porn, masturbation, and sex? Why didn't the endless hours of reality TV and movies quench the thirst of my soul? Even my husband (then boyfriend) could only fill the void temporarily.

I had been deceived. I had been lied to, tricked into believing that life was about me and joy came in the form of happiness. Happiness was "Kree getting her way or no way." But who was I to impose my desires on others? Who was I to demand my way? What if everyone got their way? Whose way is right, and whose way is wrong? I find that most of the conflict in the world results from differing ways and wills trying to be the only way. Man can't possibly know the best way. After all, humans are imperfect beings influenced by their selfish desires. You can sprinkle on top of that a few philanthropic ideals and actions, but at our core, we have been trained to care the most about ourselves.

My lack of faith in humanity to identify "the true way" turned me to the path of God—someone so much more powerful and higher than any creature on this planet. Eventually I realized that nothing was more important than getting to know my Creator. I sought God, and what I found changed my life forever.

My heart is overwhelmed with joy at the opportunity to spend an eternity with him. My mind is overwhelmed at the thought of being here another forty to fifty years in this broken, evil, sinful place. My flesh is overwhelmed with the desire to choose comfort, ease, and my selfish desires.

War.

Christ did not call us to live a life of happiness on the earth. If he is the example, look to his life! He did not live a life of luxury and comfort, praise and prestige. He had no home to lay his head down within. Even his family didn't believe him, and one of his closest friends betrayed him. His own people killed him. Look at his followers—they also suffered persecution for the love of Christ; they were beaten, stoned, exiled, and killed.

Whose happy, fuzzy, warm-feeling gospel do we listen to? The one where our life is better as we get more blessings for blessing others? The one where God touches everything we want to do and we are successful in life? The one in which we have a home, money, anything we could want? The one in which we are promised that our selfish desires, wants, and dreams *will* come true if we trust God? What kind of God are we serving when our goals, desires, and dreams overshadow his desire for a deep and intimate relationship of love, a love that sacrifices for the one who loves us the most, who showed that love by leaving his throne to teach his creation what love really is?

We are utterly, hopelessly broken, damaged, and destined for destruction without God. The fact that we can even have a relationship with him is his grace. We have done nothing to deserve this relationship and have the audacity to believe that we don't need it.

War.

These are perilous times. Times filled with fear, anxiety, stress—Satan's breeding ground for doubt, lies, temptations, and sin. To feed off the fear of uncertainty and loss of control. To pit neighbor against neighbor and son against father, destroy relationships, wreak havoc, cause chaos. Yes, the time is ripe for dissension, factions, overindulgence, anger, greed, pride. The harvest is ripe for discord and unity.

War.

I find that I am calmest when I remember who my Savior is, what he went through, and what he has given me so that I don't only survive the war but experience an overwhelming victory. You see, I may lose my job, relationships, and possessions; my body will die one day—but no one can take away my relationship with him. My trials and tribulations don't change who Jesus is or the promises he has made. My hardships and struggles do not null the joy and hope to come as I spend eternity with my Creator. Now what I see in front of me may be wicked and seem hopeless, but that doesn't change the character of God. *God is the same today and forever!* His word will not fail!

War.

I know I sound like some cliché used at your grandmother's church at 1:00 p.m. on a hot July Sunday in a little church somewhere in the backwoods of the South. Maybe I sound like that other kind of church—you know, the one with the stadium seating and lights. The one where they put on a good show but will talk about you as soon as you leave the service. Or maybe I sound like the one that is nice, generally encourages you to do good, and gives shout-outs to the politicians "visiting" around election time. The one that preaches the same three "life betterment" lessons but leaves you seriously lacking in your knowledge of God and his word. No, I'm not saying all churches are like this, but for those who think this way, know it is true that no matter the experience you have had, God doesn't change. No matter how people have treated you, his word remains the same. Whether or not you were fed the full truth of his word, he is still there waiting for you to choose to grow closer to him. Don't let the enemy keep you from the *only* one that can save you. Don't let him deceive you into thinking you have life figured out and are "good" because life will show you how horribly wrong you are in the most intense way, and it may be too late.

War.

It's like I am a soldier about to fight in the war. I get ready to leave my base to fight but don't know where I'm going or how to get there. I may have a vague idea from what one of the commanders has said, but I don't truly understand what they are saying or know what I'm doing. Also, I can't be sure that what they are saying is right. They could be paraphrasing the instructions for how to operate my weapons. Perhaps they have not given me all the instructions. I don't know because I haven't taken the time to figure out what I'm doing, where I'm going, and how to fight.

War.

So what are we going to do about this? There is a war that rages around us. A war that started in the Garden of Eden and has continued until this present time. A war that will not be silenced until Jesus has returned for his faithful servants. I know I don't want to be on the wrong side when he returns or stand before him after death having lived an unfaithful life.

This is not a game. There is a war for your soul!

This is what we have been preparing for. The day we have been waiting for.

CHAPTER 9

WEAKNESS

Fatigue, loneliness, anxiety, fear—I thought Christians were not supposed to be depressed.

If Jesus is truly enough and all of my hope and joy, why do I feel this way? What's wrong with me?

I don't have time to have depression.

Kree ponders what her doctor has told her after they finish their video appointment.

For months, she has been experiencing unexplained tiredness. Sometimes she can pinpoint the source, and other times she cannot. Her lab results also reveal that she hasn't been eating enough, not getting enough nutrients. *I thought I was OK*, she thinks to herself. *I gained twenty-five-plus pounds after separating from the military and have lost a few of those pounds. I still feel like I'm overweight.*

The doctor asked her one question she can't shake off: "Are you depressed?"

"No," she immediately replied. *Depressed?* she thought. *I can't be depressed. I don't have time to be depressed. I don't need another problem in my life.*

She looks at her phone and searches "High-functioning depression." Tears swell in her eyes as most if not all symptoms of this disease are things she is experiencing. The article calls it "PDD" and explains that people are diagnosed when they experience the symptoms for a minimum of two years. *Two years? Have I been depressed for two years and not noticed? How could I not notice that?* She feels a weight descend on her; confusion, sadness, and discouragement fill the space around her. Up to that point, she was having an OK day. She tried to spend time with God in his word and focus but couldn't for more than thirty minutes. Now she feels the weight of emptiness dragging her down.

"Lord," Kree prays, "I know that you can deliver me from anything, especially depression or anything else I may be struggling with. What's wrong with me? How did I get to this place? I don't desire to kill myself. How did I let myself get to this point?"

She sits up and tries to redirect her thoughts to more positive things. *Well, I have not been diagnosed with depression. I shouldn't self-diagnose. But what doesn't sit well with me is the fact that after I read about the symptoms of that disease, I could remember experiencing most of them. The article made sense to me—like that's what's wrong.* It feels as though she is walking through a tunnel. She can see people around her and talk. She can work. But a numbness is starting to settle in.

She wonders, *If I am depressed, when did this start?* She reflects on past experiences of sadness in high school. She saw a therapist twice but was overall able to move on. When she first entered the air force, she was alone, with no real friends. She didn't want to be in that career field and failed her initial training—a moment at which she felt really low and turned to alcohol.

Since starting her relationship with God, she has been better, but she has started to wonder whether instead of dealing with depression she has boxed it up and hidden it out of sight.

CHAPTER 10

MORE WEAKNESS

A thick blanket of jealousy covers her like a suffocating fog. As her blood pulses rapidly through her veins, she tries to combat the thoughts threatening to conquer her mind. "Why don't I get to work in a place I like, doing what I would like?"

A Kree-like figure appears in a dark purple suit of armor identical to Kree's. She smiles at Kree and says, "It's not fair. You try so hard to follow God. To make sure you are not distracted." The figure points at Alan. "He isn't doing what you are doing. Why does he get to pursue the career he wants? Why does he get to spend time doing what he wants to do? How is he supposed to disciple people while making those choices?"

Kree looks at the figure with understanding. She knows that these thoughts are not good. She knows that they are dangerous, but her emotions are so strong. "Why don't I get to do these things?"

Kree snaps out of her thoughts and gets in the car with Alan. They are on the way to visit with friends.

When they get to their friends' house, Kree notices a book on the counter: *Modern Baby Names*. Immediately Kree feels the dark, thick fog encircling her.

Cathy sees Kree with the book. "So…we are having a baby!" she exclaims.

Kree tries her hardest to look happy and supportive. "Yay!" Kree hugs Cathy and asks, "Do you know if you are having a boy or a girl yet?"

The figure in dark purple catches Kree's attention. "Really? Why do they get to have a child, but I can't? If I even try to mention having kids around Alan, he avoids the subject. Are we ever going to have kids?"

"Hey, are you OK?" Alan and Kree are headed back to their house.

Kree remains quiet for a moment, then says, "I'm trying not to be prideful."

"What's wrong, Kree?"

"I know I shouldn't compare myself to others, but I keep thinking about Cathy and Darren starting a family. Do you want kids? Are we ever going to have kids?"

Alan assesses the situation. "Do you think you are ready for a kid right now?"

"No, I guess right now isn't a good time."

"I just want to make sure that if we go that route, our child is well taken care of."

Kree looks at Alan. She is sensitive to the hardships Alan had growing up and understands why he isn't rushing to start a family. "Yeah, plus, if you are going to go back to school, we don't need a little one running around." Alan nods in agreement. "It's just that I don't like my job, and I wonder if it is OK to pursue a job that I want to do. I mean, other people do it all the time. I'm not trying to be negative, but they get to do things they like; why can't I?"

Alan looks at Kree. "Sounds like jealousy."

Kree looks at the figure in purple. What Alan says snaps her out of a trance. She can now see how the thoughts she was having were affecting her. Her glow was dimming, and she wasn't able to see the dark figure because the figure in purple was whispering in her ear. The words *covet*, *jealousy*, *bitterness*, *discontentment*, and *anger* are floating around the dark figure.

CHAPTER 11

STILL FEELING WEAK

She takes a step, a slow flow of blood dripping from her side, quickening into a steady flow. Her shield destroyed and a dagger in her hand. A hole remains where her breastplate should have shielded her from the attack. Her helmet is cracked and sliding off of her head. The amber glow in her eyes flickers—there is still hope! "Humility. If you have the courage and resolve to admit you're wrong, to admit you need help, to desire change, there is still hope…" a voice says.

She ponders what she has just read in the lesson. She has been on this journey for years now, not an expert by any means but knowledgeable about his majesty and his kingdom. She has gotten to the point where truth seems dull. Lessons feel monotonously impractical. She knows these truths and has even taught them to others. She has plateaued in her faith. Nothing seems engaging. Helpful, yes. Remindful, yes. But her passion is dissipating to a tiny flow. She is so jaded that she can't see or feel her love growing cold.

She has held on to enough faith that she feels that familiar empty feeling. The overwhelming feeling that the world has surrounded her and she has to fight her way out. The doom-filled fact that no matter how much she invests time in entertainment, her spouse, others, or success, they cannot fill her. The breath-grabbing anxiety that she is weak and can't do it. And the prevailing pride compelling her to try anyway. Some part of her knows that there is a problem. But does she care enough to figure the problem out? To get help?

Back in the Realm, gray Kree appears next to Kree. "You know so much. Their way isn't the only way. Remember, they are just people." A picture of the spiritual commander appears. "Why is he acting like you aren't trying? Why is he trying to dictate things that God doesn't dictate?"

Gray Kree looks into her eyes. "You are trying. It's not right for them to make you feel like you aren't." A picture of a spiritual army of people appears. "It's not right for them to try to make you the Christian they want you to be. They are not God."

Kree turns to her flesh. "They are just trying to help. If I didn't need help, I wouldn't have come to them in the first place. Sure, I don't agree with every decision, but it is all to help me be holy."

Gray Kree smirks. "That's true, but you're not happy there, are you? I feel every begrudged attempt to please them. You love God, I love God, but you may want to consider whether you want to stay with them."

"You know, the sad part is, you're right, at least about how I feel. I don't necessarily see myself being with them forever. If that's where God wants me, fine, but if I had another option, I would probably choose it," Kree responds.

"Do you see this arrow?" Gray Kree plunges the arrow deeper into Kree. "I bet you didn't even realize you had this wound. This wound that they helped to deepen."

Kree stumbles backward and clutches her side. Lifting her hands to her eyes, she looks in horror at the warm red blood saturating them. She looks down and notices her broken foot. *How did I not realize I was hurt like this?* she thinks. She turns to her flesh. "You know very well that they didn't do this to me. People have sacrificed a lot to love me and help me. Sure, it may not feel good to change or be corrected at times, but I know they want what's best for me."

"You! You are the one that wants to trap me in your will and his." She looks at a hooded figure in white about fifty feet away. He smiles. His pale, deadly gray face is visible beneath his white hood; darkness crouches at the corners of his mouth.

He talks to another figure in white, a smaller one, who goes to Kree and says, "You've done enough. You've already sacrificed so much. You literally gave up your career for him. They are asking too much of you; besides, they aren't God. Take it easy, just a little. You're tired, overwhelmed, stressed. Become numb to your problems; it will do you good." He points to a void that looks like a screen.

"I am tired and don't feel like thinking about anything," she says as she walks toward the void.

"You do enough; maybe you should consider whether you want to stay with them." "I…I…I'm not sure. I'm not sure if I want to stay, but I know staying is good for me."

He looks over her broken armor and wounds, then says, "Let me help you with the pain." He pulls out a large syringe and plunges it into her heart.

Kree gets a text message from a church friend. It reads, "Hey, how is your week going? How are you applying what you have been reading?" She puts her phone down and turns on the TV.

The smaller hooded figure in white returns to his master. "I tried, but she still holds on to that wretched faith. She still seeks to love God and these vermin."

His master speaks. "Oh, I would say that we have been successful today. I can't currently get her to destroy her faith through sin, which is more fun. But I can also endure her slow and agonizing defeat. I have time; I can lull her to sleep. I can have her reject her faith all while keeping her from those vermin who want to help her. Have faith in a distracted, numbed warrior for him. Oh, the ways we can keep her from her true purpose and destroy those who she could help in the meantime."

Sometime later, he appears next to her as she clutches her torso. The numbness is beginning to wear off. She can now see the blood, wounds, and holes in her armor. He points to a faint scar on her forearm.

"Remember…remember the power I have given you. Remember the free will I have given you. Remember the victories won and the enemy conquered. Your scar tells the story of such a victory."

She looks at the scar.

She is at work and receives an email from a coworker.

"You're the sorriest manager I have ever met," it reads.

She stares at the screen, shocked. "The audacity of this lady. She isn't even my boss." As she looks at the email, she can feel her cheeks flushing with anger. "If I continue to look at this, I will stay mad." She deletes the message and prepares for a work meeting.

In the Realm, a flaming arrow of anger has ricocheted off of her breastplate, but another one gets lodged into her arm.

At the meeting, her coworker tries to interrupt her. "You know what, I'm talking right now," Kree angrily exclaims. "First of all, you aren't even my boss; second of all, you need to listen to what I have to say."

A red-hooded figure smiles as if she has won a victory. Kree's demeanor has changed. The hue of her eyes is flickering between amber and brown. She is losing all peace and focus as she listens to the red-hooded figure.

"Is that the way?" a gentle voice whispers.

She speaks into the air. "She insulted me, and now she is trying to tell me what to do…it's hard not to be angry."

"Is this my way? To have your way, demand your will?"

Kree unclenches her fists. "No, it's not your way, Lord. I should have responded in love, as you would."

A translucent figure appears, of human shape but celestial design—his Spirit. The Spirit grabs her hand and leads her away from the red-hooded figure. "Remove that arrow, child. You have opened yourself to an attack. Remember that Satan can use you for his will only if you allow him to. Remove the arrow, and remove your pride. Apologize."

Several thoughts flood Kree's mind after her outburst. "I shouldn't have done that. I didn't have self-control."

"Apologize." The word appears as if out of thin air. She doesn't feel like apologizing, but she knows she needs to.

Her coworkers congratulate her on her behavior. The accuser, Carol, is very difficult to work with from anyone's perspective. They see this interaction as a victory, a successful act of putting her in her place, but this "victory" is not the example of Christ Kree wants to set. She is an ambassador for Jesus, not Satan and his plot to spread sin, anger, bitterness, and division among people.

She knocks on Carol's office door. "Hey, I wanted to talk to you about something." She walks not into the office but into the Realm.

Kree looks at her arm; a small scar has appeared where the arrow was. The arrow, now in her hand, disintegrates into the air. The translucent figure, the Spirit, starts to glow amber with intensity. "I have one last message to deliver to you before I go—from me, in 1 John 4:4, and from him, in Matthew 28:20."

She looks at the red-hooded figure and says, "I am in control of my emotions. I released the hurt, forgave, and apologized! Anger, I will not allow you to have any more power over me!"

She raises her arm and appears to squeeze the air. The figure starts gasping for breath; her hood flies off to reveal a being similar to Kree. However, her skin is pale gray, with dark veins running from her temple to the rest of her body. Kree lifts her arm higher, and the figure levitates into the air, kicking and clawing at the invisible chokehold. Suddenly, red Kree becomes limp and disintegrates into the air.

"Thank you for reminding me," Kree says as she turns to the Spirit.

"You don't have to sin. Sin is not an obligation. There is no negative emotion or thought you can't reject. I have given you a choice." The Spirit begins to fade into the air, and a familiar face briefly emerges on the translucent figure—the face of the Lord Jesus. He smiles and then disappears.

After reflecting on past victories in her faith, Kree feels motivated. She takes time to pray to and worship God. Later she feels *refreshed*. She opens up her journal and writes:

Life is not a moment in time. Life is a quest, never stopping and constantly changing.

Unpredictable, surprising, at times mundane. It's a miracle and blessing given to us. We didn't ask to be conceived; we were created and appeared. So many choices and options are available to us. Some choices bring happiness and joy; some bring sorrow and evil. Every human on the planet starts in a place. A place, an environment, a time they had no say in. Everyone is shaped and molded based on the experiences they have as they grow older. The difference between you and me is how we have chosen to respond to these experiences.

www.ingramcontent.com/pod-product-compliance
Ingram Content Group UK Ltd.
Pitfield, Milton Keynes, MK11 3LW, UK
UKHW020421250726
13967UKWH00007B/2749

9 781685 155605